WHATEVER!

by Diana G. Gallagher

illustrated by Brann Garvey

Librarian Reviewer
Laurie K. Holland
Media Specialist (National Board Certified), Edina, MN
MA in Elementary Education, Minnesota State University, Mankato

Reading Consultant
Elizabeth Stedem
Educator/Consultant, Colorado Springs, CO
MA in Elementary Education, University of Denver, CO

STONE ARCH BOOKS
MINNEAPOLIS   SAN DIEGO

Claudia Cristina Cortez is published by Stone Arch Books
151 Good Counsel Drive, P.O. Box 669
Mankato, Minnesota 56002
www.stonearchbooks.com

Copyright © 2008 by Stone Arch Books

Library of Congress Cataloging-in-Publication Data
Gallagher, Diana G.
    Whatever: The Complicated Life of Claudia Cristina Cortez / by Diana G.
Gallagher; illustrated by Brann Garvey.
    p. cm. — (Claudia Cristina Cortez)
    Summary: It seems as if the Whatever Club is doomed when Adam insists
on joining, then wants to play baseball or video games instead of reading
magazines and doing other things thirteen-year-old Claudia and her girlfriends
are used to doing.
    ISBN-13: 978-1-59889-839-2 (library binding)
    ISBN-10: 1-59889-839-6 (library binding)
    ISBN-13: 978-1-59889-880-4 (paperback)
    ISBN-10: 1-59889-880-9 (paperback)
    [1. Clubs—Fiction. 2. Friendship—Fiction. 3. Middle schools—Fiction.
4. Schools—Fiction.] I. Garvey, Brann, ill. II. Title.
PZ7.G13543Wha 2008
[Fic]—dc22   2007005954

Art Director: Heather Kindseth
Graphic Designer: Kay Fraser

Photo Credits
Delaney Photography, cover

Printed in the United States of America

Table of Contents

Cast of

ME

CLAUDIA

That's me. I'm thirteen, and I'm in the seventh grade at Pine Tree Middle School. I live with my mom, my dad, and my brother, Jimmy. I have one cat, Ping-Ping. I like music, baseball, and hanging out with my friends.

MONICA

MONICA is my very best friend. We met when we were really little, and we've been best friends ever since. I don't know what I'd do without her! Monica loves horses. In fact, when she grows up, she wants to be an Olympic rider!

BECCA

BECCA is one of my closest friends. She lives next door to Monica. Becca is really, really smart. She gets good grades. She's also really good at art.

Characters

TOMMY's our class clown. Sometimes he's really funny, but sometimes he is just annoying. Becca has a crush on him . . . but I'd never tell.

I think **PETER** is probably the smartest person I've ever met. Seriously. He's even smarter than our teachers! He's also one of my friends. Which is lucky, because sometimes he helps me with homework.

ADAM and I met when we were in third grade. Now that we're teenagers, we don't spend as much time together as we did when we were kids, but he's always there for me when I need him. (Plus, he's the only person who wants to talk about baseball with me!)

Cast of

Every school has a bully, and **JENNY** is ours. She's the tallest person in our class, and the meanest, too. She always threatens to stomp people. No one's ever seen her stomp anyone, but that doesn't mean it hasn't happened!

JENNY

ANNA

ANNA is the most popular girl at our school. Everyone wants to be friends with her. I think that's weird, because Anna can be really, really mean. I mostly try to stay away from her.

CARLY is Anna's best friend. She always tries to act exactly like Anna does. She even wears the exact same clothes. She's never really been mean to me, but she's never been nice to me either!

CARLY

Characters

NICK is my annoying seven-year-old neighbor. I get stuck babysitting him a lot. He likes to make me miserable. (Okay, he's not that bad ALL of the time . . . just most of the time.)

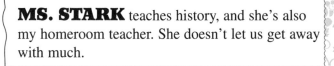

MS. STARK teaches history, and she's also my homeroom teacher. She doesn't let us get away with much.

SYLVIA's nice, but we're not that close. She thinks Anna and Carly are so cool. She doesn't realize that they're mean.

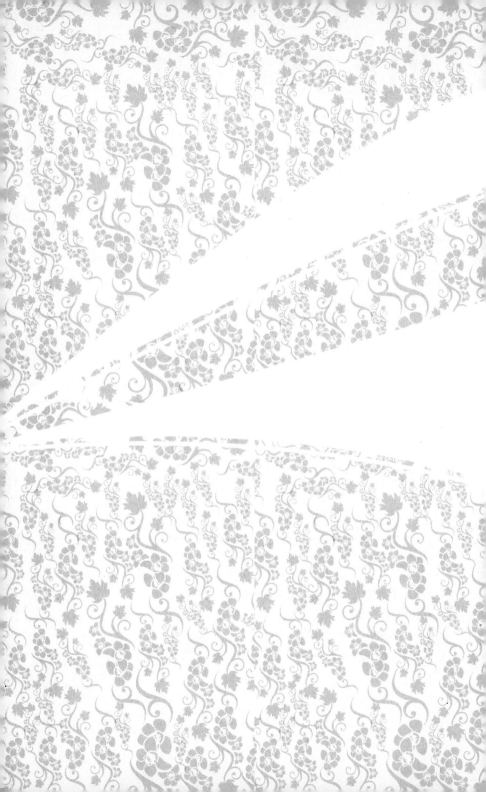

CHAPTER 1

CODE WORD: SECRETS

Lunch is the most important meal of the day. That is, if you're thirteen and a student at Pine Tree Middle School.

Our social life is TOTALLY linked to lunch. Everyone has a **favorite** table, and the same kids sit together everyday.

Lunch is the only time of the day when we can **talk, laugh,** and **pass notes** without getting into trouble.

Seventh graders have a lot to talk about.

We **complain** about homework and cram for tests.

We get EXCITED when there's a contest or something special happening.

But no matter what, the cafeteria is always buzzing with gossip.

The buzz moves faster when it's about someone.

Sometimes the gossip is true, and sometimes it isn't.

I was walking to the table I usually share with Monica and Becca when I heard someone call my name.

"Claudia, can you come here for a second?" Anna asked.

I stopped at the end of her table and stared.

Anna is the most popular girl in school. I don't know why. She's BOSSY and makes everyone sorry if she doesn't get her way. She can also be really MEAN.

Some of the mean things I've heard Anna say:

1. "Do you like wearing antique clothes?"

2. "Don't worry. Some people think ugly is cute."

3. "I didn't know they made shoes that big!"

Anna always says she's trying to help, but really, **she likes hurting people's feelings.**

I'm luckier than most people, because Anna only talks to me when she wants something.

When Anna called me over to her table, I wanted to keep walking, but I didn't.

Having Anna make fun of you is bad. It makes you wish you were invisible. Having Anna mad at you is worse. **It makes you want to move and change your name.**

"What's up, Anna?" I asked.

"You're friends with Becca, right?" Anna asked.

Carly and the other girls at the table giggled. They all belonged to Anna's club, **the Glory Girls.**

Anna knows Becca is one of my best friends. There was no reason to ask me that. Every time she sees me, I'm either with Monica or Becca, or both.

Anna was up to something, and it couldn't be good. Not for Becca and me anyway.

"Is Becca **totally in love** with Tommy?" Anna asked.

Becca ♡ Tommy

I gasped. "No! She just likes him," I said.

Anna's face lit up. She laughed and said, "Same thing."

"Not 𝕋𝕙𝔸𝕋 kind of like," I said. "Becca and Tommy are friends. He makes her laugh."

Anna rolled her eyes. "That's not what I heard."

"You heard wrong," I said.

The Claudia Cortez branch of the grapevine never spreads rumors that might be lies. I don't even tell anyone true things if the things are mean.

Anna tells everyone everything she hears.

I joined my friends at our table in the corner. I sat between Monica and Adam, **two of my best friends.**

I didn't want to upset Becca, so I didn't mention Anna's rumor.

"Want to help me sort my new baseball cards after school, Claudia?" Adam asked. "I'll give you the ones I already have."

Monica and Becca SNAPPED their heads around. They stared at me.

I looked at Adam.

Adam didn't talk to me until third grade. That's when he found out **I love** baseball. Since then, we've been really **good friends**.

We used to do everything together. Since middle school started, we don't hang out all the time, but he's still one of my best friends ever.

Baseball is still in my **Top Ten favorite things,** but I have other interests now.

"She can't," Monica blurted out.

"I can't today, Adam," I said. "I'm sorry."

Becca, Monica, and I had plans for a meeting of our club, **the Whatever Club.**

We couldn't postpone the meeting. We were going to make jewelry, and we'd been collecting jewelry supplies for a month.

"Too much HOMEWORK?" Adam asked.

I shook my head.

"Are you **working?**" Adam asked. He knows I babysit my neighbor, Nick, and do other jobs sometimes.

"No," I said. Then I tried to change the subject. "My French fries are soggy," I said. I stuffed a few of the soggy fries in my mouth anyway. Then I took a big gulp of milk.

But Adam wasn't done asking me questions. "Did you get **grounded?**" he asked. "Or is your grandma coming over for dinner? Or what?"

I just shrugged. The Whatever Club isn't exactly a secret, but Monica, Becca, and I are the only members.

If we told Adam about the meeting, **he might feel left out.**

On the other hand, I knew he wouldn't want to make jewelry with us.

Tommy stopped at our table. "Got room for me?" he asked.

His lunch tray was balanced on his head. Tommy is the class clown, but **he's not always as funny as he thinks he is.** His milk carton started to slide.

"Sure, have a seat," Becca said.

Tommy's tray tipped, and the milk carton fell off. Becca shrieked and pushed her chair back.

I threw my arm over my face. **I didn't want to be splattered.**

But the carton didn't break. Tommy picked it up and tossed it to Monica.

Monica squealed and fumbled the carton. Then she threw it back to Tommy. "It's **empty**!" she exclaimed.

Tommy laughed and sat down.

Adam didn't laugh. He pushed limp French fries around his plate with his fork.

Tommy grinned at Becca. **"Scared you, huh?"**

"Yeah!" Becca said. She giggled. They **smiled** at each other.

I looked over and saw Anna watching. She nudged Carly and pointed at Becca.

Carly looked at Becca, and then whispered something to another girl.

That girl whispered something to someone else.

And the Becca and Tommy romance rumor started flying.

CODE WORD: ANNA

After school, Becca and Monica waited for me by the front steps. Sometimes Adam waits with them, but he wasn't there today.

"You are going to LOVE my jewelry-making stuff," Becca said.

"Don't tell me!" Monica said, covering her ears. "I want to be **surprised.** Don't you, Claudia?"

"Absolutely!" I agreed.

I had a SURPRISE, too. My mom had found a bunch of old necklaces at a thrift store. She gave them to me, and I thought they would be **perfect.** We could take them apart and use the beads and stones to make new pieces of jewelry.

"This is going to be the best **Whatever Club** meeting ever," Becca said.

"The Whatever Club," Anna said. She laughed meanly. She had snuck up behind us.

Becca, Monica, and I spun around.

"That's the worst name for a club ever," Anna said. She made a face like she had just bit into a lemon.

Like I said, **the Whatever Club** isn't a secret. We just don't talk about it with anyone else, especially Anna.

Anna thinks everything she does is better than anything anyone else does. That includes clubs.

Anna started the **Glory Girls** during the first week of sixth grade. We were all thrilled to be in middle school. But things weren't as great as we thought they'd be.

All the girls wanted to be in Anna's club. Even Becca, Monica, and me. But Anna only let her **close friends** join.

Anna, Carly, and their friends = the COOL **kids**

Everyone else = EVERYONE ELSE

Our feelings were hurt. Really, **really hurt.** So Becca and Monica and I started our own club.

"A club should be about something," Anna went on. "Like the school cooking club or the dance club."

Adam belongs to the model car club at 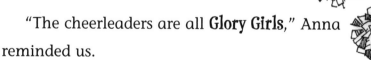 school, but he likes to build spaceships, too. Peter and the other brainy kids are in the science club.

"The baseball team," Becca said.

Anna **rolled her eyes.** "Sports teams are not clubs."

"But all the athletes hang out together like a club," Becca said.

"So do the cheerleaders," Monica said.

"The cheerleaders are all **Glory Girls**," Anna reminded us.

"The Glory Girls aren't about something," Monica said. She's 𝕊𝕋𝕌𝔹𝔹𝕆ℝℕ. She didn't want Anna to have the last word.

"We are too," Anna said. Her eyes flashed. "The Glory Girls are about being **cool** and POPULAR and **keeping up with all the latest styles.**"

"Do you watch **MyWorld?**" Becca asked. She was trying to be nice. "That's our favorite TV show. We watch it together every week."

"The Glory Girls is NOTHING like your club," Anna said. She sounded insulted. "**The Whatever Club** doesn't have any purpose at all. You don't even have a regular meeting day! The Glory Girls meet once a week and we have a reason for existing," she said with a mean look on her face.

"We have meetings when we have a reason," I explained.

"Doing whatever we want whenever we want," Monica said.

"Who's in charge?" Anna asked.

"NOBODY. We vote on everything," Becca said. "And all our decisions have to be **unanimous.**"

Monica nodded. "If we don't all agree, we don't do it," she explained.

"Whatever it is," I added.

YES	NO!
|||	O

"The **Glory Girls** do what I want," Anna said.

It's funny how things work out sometimes.

Monica, Becca, and I were **really upset** when Anna wouldn't let us be **Glory Girls**.

When it happened, I couldn't sleep.

But that was the best thing that could have happened, because that's why **we started our own club.**

Our club is called the **WHATEVER CLUB** because we couldn't agree on one thing the club should be about. We're interested in more than one thing, of course!

We take turns choosing different things to do, and we are never bored.

But the **best thing** about the **Whatever Club** is that **Anna can't boss us around.**

CHAPTER 3

CODE WORD: BAD NEWS

The **Whatever Club** meets in different places. Sometimes we go to the mall to see movies or to Pizza Plaza for pizza.

Usually, though, we meet in the tree house in my backyard.

That's not as BORING as it sounds. My dad built the tree house for my brother when he was seven. Jimmy is sixteen now and doesn't use it anymore, so we do.

The Cortez tree house isn't a little kid's play fort. **It's a house.** The tree house has two glass windows. A large tree grows through a hole in the middle. We can stand up without hunching over, and the roof doesn't leak.

We keep the club journal, cushions, and other  supplies inside wooden benches. The benches are built into the walls of the tree house.

My jewelry supplies were piled on a bench.

Ping-Ping, my pet cat, was asleep on the windowsill.

There's only one bad thing about the tree house. The **Whatever Club** wasn't the only thing that moved in when Jimmy moved out.

Now, **lots of little animals** live in the tree house.

BIRDS build nests in the corners.

SQUIRRELS race up and down the tree trunk. They also leave acorn shells on the floor.

Feathers and fur don't bother Becca and Monica, but I have to sweep out the **spider webs** before our meetings.

I'm glad that my friends don't know that **some snakes can climb trees** looking for insects and bird eggs to eat.

I've never found a snake in the tree house, but I don't want my friends to know it's a possibility.

I heard Becca and Monica in the back yard.

Monica yelled up, "Are all the **creepy crawlies** gone?"

I looked out the door. Monica and Becca were both carrying shopping bags.

"Yes!" I yelled back.

Monica and Becca climbed the ladder.

"This meeting of the **Whatever Club is open!**" I announced. "Today's code word is **Jewelry.**" All our meetings have a word or words that describe what we're doing.

Becca **scribbled in the club journal.** It was her idea to keep notes about our meetings. Sometimes she writes a lot. Today she just wrote down the date and code word. Then she put the notebook down.

"Wait until you see this!" Becca said. She looked excited as she pulled a string of pearls out of her bag. I was sure they weren't real, but they were really BEAUTIFUL.

"Oh, that's **gorgeous!**" Monica exclaimed. "What else did you bring?"

"More beads!" Becca held up two boxes of beads. She also had dangling clip-on earrings, necklaces, and bracelets her mom found at garage sales.

Each of us had some beading wire and a pair of pliers.

Monica had a bunch of necklace clasps.

I had a box of my mom's old jewelry that she didn't want anymore.

We sat down on the floor and began creating our jewelry.

I waited until our meeting was almost over to tell the terrible thing I knew.

Bad news is bad news no matter how or when you tell it. There's NEVER a good time.

"Anna thinks you like Tommy, Becca," I said.

Becca gasped. "She does?"

"Why does she think that?" Monica asked.

"I don't know," I said. "I told Anna it wasn't true, but she didn't believe me."

"Well . . ." Becca began. Her cheeks turned red. "I do sort of like Tommy **more than a friend,**" she admitted.

Monica and I were shocked. We looked at each other. Then we stared at Becca.

"But I don't want anyone else to know," Becca added.

"We won't tell," Monica promised her.

That's another great thing about the **Whatever Club.** We never tell each other's SECRETS. Not to ANYONE.

Not ever, for any reason.

After our meeting, Becca and Monica left the tree house first.

I made sure the tree house was clean. I swept up a few small beads that we hadn't picked up, and I gathered up the empty soda cans. Then I headed down the ladder.

Adam was waiting by the bottom of the ladder when I climbed down.

I could tell he was sad the second I saw him. "Hey, Adam," I said. "What are you doing here?"

Adam looked down at the ground. Then he looked up at the tree house. Finally, he looked me in the eye.

"Don't you like me anymore, Claudia?" Adam asked.

CHAPTER 4

CODE WORD: ODD MAN OUT

My feelings were hurt. I couldn't believe Adam thought I didn't like him anymore. Adam and I are closer than **dogs and fleas, thunder and lightning, or hamburgers and fries.**

Okay, so we've had a few fights.

I'm still annoyed at Adam for putting a toad on my plate at our fourth-grade picnic.

Another time, I outbid him for an autographed baseball in an auction online. He didn't speak to me for days. He felt like a JERK when I gave him the ball for his birthday.

But how could he possibly think I didn't like him?

"Why do you think that?" I asked.

"Because you didn't want to come over," Adam explained. "I know you still collect baseball cards."

Then Nick, my 𝔸ℕℕ𝕆𝕐𝕀ℕ𝔾 neighbor, ran out of the back door of my house. He ran right up to Adam and me.

"Claudia doesn't like me, either," Nick said. "But **I don't care.**"

Nick lives next door. My mom watches him when his mother has something to do. I can't stand him. Sometimes I think **his mom can't stand him, either. She goes out a lot.**

"Go watch TV, Nick," I said.

"Yeah, Nick," Adam said.

All my friends know Nick and wish they didn't.

Nick throws 𝕋𝔸ℕ𝕋ℝ𝕌𝕄𝕊, wrecks stuff, lies, and tattles. Most people have good and bad points, but I can only think of one good thing about Nick: My friends put up with him, and **that proves they really like me.**

"Claudia's mom made me come out here." Nick glared at Adam. "Baseball cards are STUPID."

"Some baseball cards are worth **a lot of money,**" I said. "Now go away."

"There's nothing to do in your yard," Nick said.

"Catch bugs," I said.

Mom used to keep toys at our house for Nick. She stopped when she saw him smash a plastic truck with a rock. **He told her my cat sat on it.**

Nick went away when Adam gave him a **quarter.**

"I know you can't spend all your **free time with me,**" Adam said. "But we don't spend **ANY** time together."

I didn't know what to say.

When we were little, I **LOVED** playing with Adam.

I didn't mind crawling around in the dirt looking for pirate treasure. **Dirty knees didn't bother me.**

I liked building forts, making castles with plastic blocks, and playing baseball. I still like playing baseball.

But I'm **thirteen now,** not nine. I like doing other things, too.

Ping-Ping crept through the grass, stalking a bird.

"Look out!" Nick shouted. He ran across the yard waving a stick. "It's the **mutant cat from Planet Z!** You can't get away from Viper Man."

"Stop that, Nick!" I yelled.

Ping-Ping knows all about the **mutant brat from planet Earth**. She dashed for the house and zoomed in the pet door.

Nick didn't follow the cat. **He whacked the tops off dandelions with his stick.**

Adam and I sat on the bench by my mother's rose garden.

"We haven't played catch in weeks," Adam said.

"I know." I sighed. "I've been busy."

"I don't get much practice with Tommy or Peter," Adam said. "Peter's smart, but he's not a very good ball player. And **Tommy clowns around too much.**"

"Here's the bug you told me to catch, Claudia!" **Nick dropped a beetle down the back of my shirt.**

The bug's scratchy feet tap-danced down my spine.

I'm not scared of bugs or toads. But I don't want them in my clothes!

Nick laughed when I squealed and jumped up. I shook my shirt and jiggled until the bug dropped on the ground.

Adam frowned at Nick. "That wasn't very nice."

"I wasn't trying to be nice!" Nick yelled.

He stomped on Adam's shoe, and then ran.

"Believe me, Adam," I said. "I'd rather play catch with you than do homework or chores or watch Nick, but I can't be in two places at once."

"I know." Adam looked me in the eye. **"That's why I want to join the Whatever Club."**

CHAPTER 5

CODE WORD: OH, BOY

We don't have club meetings two days in a row very often, but this was an EMERGENCY.

"We have a PROBLEM. I'm calling a **Whatever Club** meeting," I told Becca and Monica at lunch.

"What problem?" Becca asked.

"I absolutely **cannot talk about it here,**" I whispered. "The code word is BOY."

Becca gasped and lowered her voice. "Did Tommy hear Anna's rumor? Does he know I sort of like him?"

"No, that's not it," I said.

"Is it about Brad?" Monica asked. "Did he talk to you? Did you faint?"

"No, no, and no." I rolled my eyes. "I called a **Whatever Club** meeting because we can't talk about it here."

"Talk about what?" Tommy asked.

He dropped his tray on the table and sat down. Adam sat down beside him.

"Uh. Well, um . . ." Becca stammered.

"Nothing," Monica said. "What's new with you, Tommy?"

Tommy frowned.

That was new. **Tommy is always clowning around and cracking jokes.**

"Do I smell bad?" Tommy asked. **"Am I going bald?"**

"You're too young to go bald," Monica said.

"Why?" I asked.

"Everybody's looking at me FUNNY and GIGGLING," Tommy said. "Except I'm not trying to make them **laugh.**"

Anna isn't just **bossy** and **selfish.** She has a BIG MOUTH. The rumor about Becca and Tommy was moving through the school at the **speed of light.**

* * *

Becca was still upset when she got to the tree house after school. **"Sooner or later someone's going to tell Tommy I like him,"** she said. She looked worried.

"Would that be so bad?" Monica asked.

"Are you kidding?" Becca looked SHOCKED. "What if Tommy doesn't like me back? He might not even want to be friends any more."

"If Tommy hears the rumor, we'll just tell him **Anna started it,**" I said. "Then he won't think it's true."

"Will that work?" Becca looked hopeful.

"Yes," I said. "Our **other boy problem** won't be so easy to fix."

"What other boy problem?" both girls asked at once.

"Adam wants to join the **Whatever Club,**" I said.

"But he's a BOY!" Monica exclaimed.

"We don't have **a no-boy rule,**" I said. "It wouldn't be fair to keep him out because of that. Remember, we started the Whatever Club because Anna wouldn't let us join the **Glory Girls.**"

"But this is different." Becca looked upset again.

"Yeah," Monica said. "We talk about stuff I don't want anyone else to know, **especially a boy!**"

"You and Becca know all my secrets," Monica said.

Monica's secrets aren't terrible. She sleeps with the light on, and she kept every Valentine she's ever gotten. Her dream is to be an Olympic rider.

My secret is a little bit more embarrassing. **I would absolutely die if everyone knew I had a crush on Brad Turino.**

He's a GORGEOUS sports star. He's also the only person in the universe I can't talk to without stuttering.

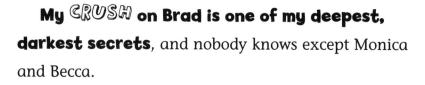

My CRUSH on Brad is one of my deepest, darkest secrets, and nobody knows except Monica and Becca.

If Adam joined the **Whatever Club,** he'd probably find out. He wouldn't tell anyone, but he'd tease me.

"You know all my secrets, too," Becca said.

"We didn't tell Anna that you like Tommy." Monica held up her right hand. "I don't know how she found out."

"She probably saw me staring at him and guessed," Becca said.

"Or she made it up to be MEAN," I said. "Anna doesn't know it's true."

Monica changed the subject. "Why does Adam want to join our club?"

"Because I've been with you and Becca so much lately," I explained.

"Baking cookies for the school bake sale," Becca said.

"And babysitting together for EXTRA CASH," Monica added.

"But we still have to water-seal the tree house so it doesn't rot," I argued. **"Adam would be a really big help."**

"We don't have to talk about embarrassing things when Adam's around," Becca said.

We voted.

Finally, we agreed to let Adam join the Whatever Club for a TWO-WEEK **trial period.**

CHAPTER 6

CODE WORD: WELCOME

I told Adam the good news the next day after school as we walked to my house. "We voted to give you a trial membership," I said.

"I'm in?" Adam asked. "REALLY? Did everyone vote for me?"

I nodded. "Everything we do in the **Whatever Club** has to be **unanimous,**" I explained. "That's our only rule."

"This is so cool!" Adam grinned.

"If you don't like it after the two weeks are up, you don't have to join," I said.

After the two weeks were over, Becca, Monica, and I could also vote to keep him out. I didn't mention that.

"You've always liked doing stuff with me, Claudia," Adam said. "So **why wouldn't I like it?**"

The Whatever Club does some things Adam would like, and a lot of things he wouldn't.

But at least I'd be doing everything with all my BEST FRIENDS.

* * *

"This meeting of the **Whatever Club** is now open," I said. "The code word is . . ." I paused.

Then Becca, Monica, and I all shouted together. **"Welcome to the Whatever Club, Adam!"**

Adam smiled. "Thanks," he said. He sat on a bench with his hands folded.

Becca opened a small cooler. "Want a soda, Adam?" she asked.

"Sure." Adam took a cola and popped the top.

Monica held out a dish. "Have a brownie."

"Okay." Adam took a brownie. Then he sat with the soda in one hand and the brownie in the other.

"Monica makes great brownies, Adam," I said. "Try it."

"Okay." Adam took a bite and a sip, but he still looked STIFF and UNCOMFORTABLE. I was starting to feel **uncomfortable** too.

Nobody said anything. Becca stared at the floor. Monica nibbled her brownie. They were acting like the code word was NO FUN.

I tried to break the tense mood. "Did everyone bring their **knitting needles?**" I asked.

Becca's eyes widened. "Were we supposed to bring knitting needles?"

"What are knitting needles?" Monica asked.

"You know, needles for knitting," I said. "My grandma uses them to make sweaters."

Adam's face went white. "I am not going to knit," he said.

"Neither are we," I said with a laugh. "I was just trying to get you all to loosen up."

Adam set down his soda and brownie and waved his limp arms. **"I'm loose! I'm loose!"**

Becca giggled.

"Don't scare me like that, Claudia," Monica said.

"We could play a game," I suggested. Everyone agreed, and I opened the bench where we kept the games.

"You're the new guy, Adam. You pick," Monica said.

Adam wanted to play dominoes. Becca kept score, because she never forgets to write anything down.

Dominoes are on my list of favorite games. I like it because you need to have both luck and smarts to win. Luck determines what tiles you draw, but the score depends on how you play them. That's called strategy.

At the end of the first round, Becca was losing.

Adam laughed and said, **"Sorry, Becca. There's no way you can win now."**

"That's okay," Becca said. "I like playing even when I lose."

"Playing the game is what's FUN," Monica said.

"I play to WIN," Adam said.

By the end of the game we could tell that Adam plays to win any way he can. **He doesn't break the rules, but he never gives anyone a break.**

Adam beat us fair and square . . . by sixty-four points!

CODE WORD: ADAM'S CHOICE

The **Whatever Club** had NEVER met three days in a row before. The only time we ever had three meetings in one week was back in September, when we were training for the Charity Fun Run. Sometimes we only meet once every two weeks.

Monica and Becca have homework and families, too. **They're just as busy as I am.** Things we have to do stop us from doing all the things we want to do. **"Life gets in the way,"** as my mom likes to say.

But we forgot to tell Adam that we don't meet every day.

On Monday at lunch, Adam called his first meeting. The code word was BASEBALL.

Monica waited until we left the cafeteria to complain. "I hate baseball," she said.

"Our next meeting was supposed be a **WORK** meeting," Becca said. "To put water seal on the tree house."

"I know, but Adam really needs to practice batting," I said. **"We should help him out."**

Becca and Monica aren't very good baseball players, but they're really **good sports**. We agreed to help Adam practice this one time.

We met at my house after school.

I pitched. I don't throw super fast, but I always throw in the strike zone.

Becca played outfield. She only caught a few of the balls Adam hit. She said chasing the ones that got away was **GOOD EXERCISE**.

Monica caught all the pitches Adam missed and threw the ball back to me underhand. **Adam didn't tease her.** He was just glad to have a practice team.

It wasn't the PERFECT Whatever Club meeting, but it was OKAY.

* * *

Two days later, I called the monthly **Mag** meeting.

"What does **Mag** stand for?" Adam asked.

"Magazine," I explained. "I just got this month's issue of Miss Magazine."

"I subscribe to Teen Scene," Monica said.

"And I get **Boutique**," Becca finished.

"We meet every month to read them," Monica went on.

Adam looked disgusted. "I'm not going to read girl magazines. I'm a guy. Besides, if anyone found out, they'd make fun of me for months!"

I was caught in the middle. Adam was on one side and Becca and Monica were on the other. I decided to wait and see what happened at the meeting.

After school, we met at the **tree house**.

Monica and Becca brought their new issues of **Teen Scene** and **Boutique**. But Adam wouldn't vote to read magazines. He wanted to **play video games.**

Becca, Monica, and I had never broken the UNANIMOUS RULE, and we didn't want to start. Part of our club was about all of us agreeing.

Adam wouldn't change his mind. So I finally changed my vote. I voted with Adam.

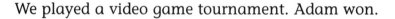

Becca SCRIBBLED something in the club journal. She showed it to Monica. Monica sighed. **"Fine,"** she said. "Video games it is."

We played a video game tournament. Adam won.

After everyone left, I was curious about why Monica had changed her mind. I opened the club journal and found Becca's note.

It said: **"Only nine more days."**

I knew what that meant. There were only nine more days before Adam's trial membership was over.

Then, if we didn't vote unanimously to let him join, **Adam would be out of the Whatever Club.**

* * *

The next day we didn't talk and laugh as much at lunch.

Everyone had an excuse:

1. Tommy heard a rumor that Anna liked him. He couldn't decide if that was good or bad.

2. Becca was glad Tommy didn't know she liked him.

3. Becca was worried that Tommy liked Anna.

4. Monica had trouble sleeping.

5. I was worried about keeping everyone in the Whatever Club happy.

When in doubt, call a meeting. I used the code word 𝕋𝕍. We met at my house after school.

"What are we going to watch?" Adam asked.

"MyWorld," I said. Everyone loves that show, even boys. It is about everything. **Movies, music, fashion, gadgets, and whatever else is cool.**

"That works," Adam said. Becca and Monica sighed with relief.

Jimmy and I don't have TV sets in our rooms, and my parents' room is off limits. So my friends and I can only watch TV in the living room. And I didn't know Mom would be watching Nick again.

"I don't want to watch this dumb show," Nick said. "*DINOSAUR JUNGLE* is on."

Nick stamped his foot and folded his arms. He stuck out **his lower lip and frowned**. I started the tantrum countdown in my head.

"I love that movie," Adam said. "Let's watch that instead of **MyWorld**."

Becca and Monica exchanged a glance.

Nick looked at me. "I want *DINOSAUR JUNGLE*!" he yelled.

The battle was on.

If we didn't change the channel, Nick would flop on the floor, *KICK*, and *CRY*. If that didn't work, he'd shriek. He wouldn't stop until he got what he wanted. Even if I tried to ignore him, Mom would make me give in. I voted with Adam and Nick to watch **Dinosaur Jungle.**

Becca looked away. Then she said, "Oh! I forgot. I have to help my mom weed the garden."

Monica yawned. "I think I need a nap," she said.

THEY LEFT.

It was my house, so I couldn't leave. I had to wait until the movie was over.

After Adam went home, I walked over to Becca's house. She and Monica live next door to each other. I peeked in the front window.

Becca wasn't weeding her mom's garden.

Monica wasn't sleeping.

They were in Becca's living room watching *MyWorld*.

This was a gazillion times worse than when Adam thought I didn't like him.

Monica and Becca had NEVER kept a secret from me, except for birthday presents and fun surprises. They had never snuck off and left me out, either.

Until now.

CHAPTER 8

CODE WORD: NO

The next morning, Monica and Becca stopped me outside the school.

"It's too hard to talk at lunch," Monica said. **"The boys are always there."**

"And we have to tell you something," Becca added.

I didn't say anything. **I was still sad and mad because they ditched me yesterday.** If they were sorry, I didn't want to mess up a chance to **FIX** our problem.

"I asked my mom to record **MyWorld** yesterday," Monica said. "Just in case."

"And we watched it together," Becca admitted.

"We didn't want you to know we were mad," Monica said.

"We were **MAD** because you voted with Adam again," Becca explained.

"We can't ask you to choose between Adam and us," Monica finished.

But I knew that was what I might have to do.

Choose.

I thought about the problem all day long.

Adam had used our UNANIMOUS RULE for selfish reasons.

Monica and Becca had voted for his activities to make me happy. Now I had to make things right with them.

At lunch I called another meeting of the Whatever Club. The code word was **Old News**.

After school, Adam helped me sweep leaves out of the tree house. We caught the spiders and let them go in Mom's garden. **Ping-Ping tried to catch them, but they escaped.**

Becca and Monica got to the tree house just after Adam and I climbed back up.

Becca had the club journal open. "What does OLD NEWS stand for?" she asked.

"Last week's gossip?" Monica guessed. "Did something **outrageous** happen and I missed it?"

"I want to read the magazines we didn't read at our REGULAR magazine meeting," I explained. The magazines were still stacked in a corner of the tree house. I got up and picked them up.

Becca and Monica looked **confused**. Adam looked upset. He crossed his arms and frowned. "I'm not voting to read magazines," he said.

"Well, we have a **Mag** meeting every month," I said. "It's a **Whatever Club tradition.** All in favor of reading magazines, raise your hands."

Becca, Monica, and I raised our hands.

"All in favor of baseball!" Adam said, raising his hand. He looked at me, but my hand was down.

"I know you'd rather **play baseball**, Claudia," Adam said.

Some days, that was true. Today I had to make a point. I had to show Adam he wasn't being fair.

"I really want to **read magazines**," I said.

"Dominoes," Adam suggested.

"Magazines," I said.

"Water-seal the tree house." Adam  smiled. He knew we wanted his help with that job.

"Not dressed for it," Becca said.

"**Nice try**, though," Monica added.

"Magazines," I said again.

Adam and I were locked in a contest of wills. I knew him so well I could predict his next move. He'd try to think of something he liked that Becca and Monica couldn't resist.

"Let's go scare Nick!" Adam exclaimed.

"𝕹𝕺𝕿𝕳𝕴𝕹𝕲 scares Nick," Monica said.

"But we could try," Becca said. "Tomorrow."

Adam frowned. He wasn't mad at Becca and Monica. He was mad at me because I  wouldn't give in this time.

"I'm not voting for magazines," Adam said.

I stood my ground, too. "It's magazines or NOTHING," I said.

"I agree," Monica said.

"Same here," Becca said.

"Then I guess this meeting is over." Adam stood up and left without saying goodbye.

"What if we never agree on anything ever again?" Monica asked. **"What good is a club that doesn't do anything?"**

"We might as well not have a club," Becca said.

I sighed. My plan had totally backfired. I thought Adam would see my point.

This day was not going well.

1. Adam was mad at me.

2. Monica and Becca were upset.

3. And the **Whatever Club** was doomed.

CODE WORD: CRISIS

Becca, Monica, and I had to talk about Adam. I decided to call an emergency meeting of the **Whatever Club** that wasn't exactly a meeting of the **Whatever Club.**

Here's why:

1. No code word.

2. Permanent members only.

3. Not at the tree house.

I didn't want Becca to take notes, and I didn't want Adam to find out.

But something happened every time I tried to give Monica and Becca the info.

Monica had to go back to her locker.

Becca left a book in math.

Tommy, **Peter**, and **Adam** walked with us to lunch and followed us to fifth period English.

I finally wrote a note. It said:

Roaring Rock. 4:00.

Jenny Pinski sits between Becca and me in English. I keep my backpack under my desk, my elbows in, and my eyes straight ahead. I don't want to invade her space.

The tiniest things make Jenny explode. Once she yelled at Peter for half an hour because he bumped into her.

When we choose teams in GYM CLASS, Jenny is always the first one picked because no one wants to make her mad. Not even Anna.

This time **I had to risk it.** I held the note out behind Jenny's back. Then I signaled Becca. "PSSSST!"

Before Becca heard me, Jenny looked around. She yanked the note out of my hand.

I stopped breathing.

Jenny unfolded the paper and read it. "Is this about **your club**?" she asked.

I was so NERVOUS I couldn't answer.

"I'll be there," Jenny said.

I nodded. "Okay," I whispered.

I felt numb. Adam wasn't the **Whatever Club's** biggest problem now.

I finally got Becca and Monica alone after school. "Jenny Pinski thinks **I invited her to the Whatever Club meeting**," I said.

"What meeting?" Monica asked.

"The one I told you about in the note that Jenny took," I said. "Roaring Rock at 4 o'clock."

Becca GASPED. Then she grabbed my arm. "You have to tell Jenny it's CANCELLED."

"You think I should un-invite Jenny?" I said, shocked. **I arched my eyebrow.** I do that when something sounds odd or crazy.

Becca saw my look and shrugged. "Not a good idea, huh?" she asked.

I SHOOK my head.

Anna gets her way because nobody wants to make the most POPULAR girl at Pine Tree Middle School mad. Jenny gets her way because **nobody wants to get stomped.**

"What are we going to do?" Monica asked.

"Come to Roaring Rock ten minutes early," I said. "I have a plan and a **secret weapon.**"

* * *

Roaring Rock is a climbing boulder in the park. I was already there when Becca and Monica arrived.

"Okay, what's the plan?" Becca asked.

"We have to make Jenny decide she doesn't want to join the Whatever Club," I explained.

Monica and Becca raised their eyebrows. My idea did sound CRAZY.

Nick ran up and sat on the rock. "Tie my shoe, Claudia."

"What's he doing here?" Monica scowled at Nick.

"He's our secret weapon," I said.

Mom was shocked when I offered to take Nick to the park. Usually I hate taking him to the playground. He BULLIES other kids and throws a fit when it's time to leave.

He was also our only hope of saving the Whatever Club from Jenny Pinski.

Jenny arrived right on time.

"We're so glad you came," Becca said.

That was a lie, but we didn't want to hurt Jenny's feelings. **Or get punched**.

"Yeah, right," Jenny said. She didn't look like she believed us. "What do you do in this club?"

"We make money," I explained.

"Mostly by babysitting brats no one else wants to watch," Monica said. She pointed at Nick. "Like that one."

Nick held out a caterpillar and chased a little girl.

"We make two dollars an hour," I told Jenny.

Then I shouted at Nick, "Stop that right now, Nick!"

Nick stopped and **stuck out his tongue.** Then he went back to chasing the little girl.

"Let's go," I said. "We can't let him tease all the little kids."

We all ran to the little girl's rescue.

Jenny stepped in front of Nick. "Knock it off, kid."

"Or what?" Nick said. He put his hands on his hips.

Jenny's eyes narrowed. **"Or you'll be very sorry."**

Monica, Becca, and I watched from the sidelines.

It was just like a showdown scene in an old western movie. Except Nick and Jenny were both bad guys.

"You can't do nothing to me," Nick said. "I'm little."

Jenny blinked. Nick was right. She couldn't beat up a little kid, **even if he was horrible.**

Nick kicked Jenny in the shin.

"OW!" Jenny yelled. She grabbed her leg and hopped on one foot.

Then Nick put the caterpillar in her hair.

Jenny hopped on one foot and shook her head. "Get it out! Get it out!"

Nick doubled over LAUGHING.

Becca, Monica, and I did not laugh. We weren't little. Jenny could beat us up any time she wanted.

But **she didn't stand a chance against Nick.** It's amazing how much trouble one little kid can get into.

Nick sprayed us with water from the fountain. Then he ran away and hid.

It took Becca, Monica, and me ten minutes to find him.

After we found Nick, he tried to run away from us again, but he fell. He scraped his knee and screamed until I kissed it to make it better.

Note to self: Have Band-Aids in pocket when at park with Nick.

Nick SPIT on Monica's shoe and pulled Becca's hair. He found gum **stuck on a swing** and chewed it. Even Jenny was grossed out.

She only lasted twenty minutes.

"Oh, no!" Jenny exclaimed. "I can't join your club."

"Why not?" Becca asked.

Jenny frowned. I could tell she was trying to think up a good excuse.

I didn't care if **she had a good reason or not!**

"None of your business," Jenny said. Then she ran off.

"Oh my gosh, **it worked!**" Monica yelled. She grinned.

I was glad too. **Nick must be the only person in the world Jenny Pinski would rather avoid than stomp.** And I don't blame her.

Dirt hit the back of my neck. I turned to Nick. "I'll buy ice cream if you stop throwing sand."

A bribe is the only thing that works with Nick.

CODE WORD: CLUBS

GOOD: Jenny Pinski didn't want to join the Whatever Club.

BAD: Adam did.

We couldn't use Nick to make Adam quit. He already knew the Whatever Club was about having fun.

He also knew about the **UNANIMOUS RULE**. We couldn't make Adam do anything he didn't want to do.

And that was no fun for Becca, Monica, and me.

If Adam stayed, the **Whatever Club** wouldn't be the same.

I didn't know what to do. So I knocked on Jimmy's door. I was shocked when he opened it. Usually Jimmy doesn't really want to talk to me.

"Why'd you quit the high school gaming club?" I asked my brother. **"Didn't you like the other kids?"**

"My friends joined too," Jimmy said. "But the school computers are 𝓣𝓞𝓞 𝓞𝓛𝓓  to run the newest games. We all have better computers at home, **so we all quit.**"

"But wouldn't it be more fun to play with your friends?" I didn't need to know this. **I was just curious.**

"We play over the Internet. We don't have to be in the same room to play together," Jimmy said.

That was the longest conversation I've had with Jimmy in a month. **But it didn't help me with the Adam problem.**

Uncle Diego was watching TV in our living room.

"Did you join a club when you were kid?" I asked.

"Didn't want to," Uncle Diego said. "And no one ever asked me."

"Did Dad ever join a club?" I didn't want to wait until Dad came home from his computer store to find out.

"ＨＡ!" Uncle Diego laughed and slapped his knee. "He was always too busy studying or working to have fun. Hey, **what are we having for dinner?**"

"I'll go ask Mom," I said.

My mother was chopping up carrots in the kitchen. I sat down on one of the stools by the counter. "Mom, were you ever in a club?" I asked.

"I was the only girl in my high school chess club," Mom said.

"How many boys were in it?" I asked, reaching out to grab a carrot.

"Eight." Mom smiled. "At first, they wouldn't talk to me."

I was shocked. **"What a bunch of jerks!"** I said.

"They thought that would make me quit," Mom went on, "but it didn't. When they realized I loved the game just as much as they did, we all became good friends."

I sighed. Monica, Becca, and I couldn't stop talking to Adam. That would be mean. And I wanted to stay friends with Adam. **I couldn't risk losing him as a friend.**

After dinner, Dad took me to the field behind the driving range at the golf course. He pays fifty cents for every golf ball I find. **His odd jobs are always pretty odd.**

"I have a question about your **golf club**," I said.

"I have a bag full of clubs," Dad said. "Drivers, irons, and a putter."

"Not the clubs you use to hit balls," I said. "I meant the Country Club, where you play golf."

Dad frowned. "I almost joined the Country Club, but I didn't. Too many **boring meetings** and too many RULES."

I was confused. "But you played at the Country Club last week."

"Yes, I did," Dad said. "All my golf buddies are members, and I go as their guest. **It's the best of both worlds.**"

"What does that mean?" I asked.

Dad picked up a golf ball I missed. "I can play the golf course, but I don't have to go to the meetings."

ℍ𝕄𝕄. Maybe that could help me.

Adam had been with Becca, Monica, and me all day. But he didn't call a club meeting or ask if we were having one.

Adam was really mad because I sided with Becca and Monica about the magazines. **Maybe he had already decided to quit!**

CHAPTER 11

CODE WORD: GLORY GUYS

I talked to Adam before school the next day. He wasn't mad about my magazine vote anymore. **And he wasn't going to quit the Whatever Club.**

"I'm not going to vote for everything you want to do," I said.

"Yes, you will," Adam said. "Everything has to be unanimous. So you and Becca and Monica will vote to play baseball or build model cars or read superhero comics."

"Why would we do that?" I asked.

"Because it's better than doing nothing," Adam said.

That made me mad! **It was so** SELFISH **and unfair.**

I almost told Adam that Becca and Monica only let him in the club to help water seal the tree house.

Before I said anything, Anna walked over to us.

"Peter and Tommy are joining MY CLUB," Anna said.

"They are?" Adam asked.

"Of course! I asked five boys, and they all want to be **Glory Guys.** But you can't, Adam." Anna sneered. "You already belong to the **Whatnot Club.**"

"It's the **Whatever Club**," Adam said. "And I like it. A lot. More than being a Glory Boy."

"**Glory Guy**," Anna said.

"Whatever." Adam grinned at me as Anna walked away.

My insides felt warm. I was glad Adam would rather hang out with Becca, Monica, and me than with the cool crowd.

But that was also **the problem.**

Monica, Becca, and I walked home from school together.

"This is stupid," Monica said. "It's like we have two **Whatever Clubs.** One that meets with Adam, and one that meets in secret without him."

"This isn't really a meeting," Becca said. "NO CODE WORD."

"But it feels more like a meeting than the real meetings now," I said.

"I don't like sneaking around behind Adam's back," Monica admitted. "But **I'm tired of doing everything he wants and nothing we want.**"

"He'll never vote for our stuff, will he?" Becca asked.

I shook my head. "Nope."

"We can get our club back," Monica said. "We don't have to make Adam a permanent member."

"We might lose Adam as a friend," I said.

"And hurt his feelings," Becca said.

"He did choose us over Anna and her **Glory Guys**," I reminded them.

"I don't think Tommy and Peter will stay in Anna's club very long," Becca said. "The Glory Girls don't vote on anything. They do what Anna wants."

"Anna's club isn't fair, like ours is," Monica said. "In the **Whatever Club,** we all make the rules."

"Sort of," Becca said. "Adam only has one vote, but he still wins."

Nobody won before Adam. We all voted to do things the others liked. It evened out, just like my luck.

"I don't want to change the Unanimous Rule," Monica said. "And **I don't want to be mean to Adam.** But we have to do something or our club won't be our club anymore."

"I can't think of anything," Becca said.

"I have an idea," I said. "But **we'll have to vote Adam in as a permanent member of the Whatever Club.**"

CHAPTER 12

CODE WORD: INITIATION

I went to Adam's house and told him we voted him into the **Whatever Club** early. He was so happy he jumped up, spun, and gave me a high five.

He wasn't quite so happy when he got to the tree house later that afternoon. The code word for the meeting was INITIATION.

"You didn't tell me there was a TEST," Adam said.

"An initiation doesn't mean a test," Becca explained. "It just marks the beginning of something."

"Starting today, you'll be a **permanent member** of the **Whatever Club,**" I said.

"Right after you tell us your **deepest, darkest secret,**" Monica finished.

"What?" Adam was so surprised his voice cracked.

"We told each other our deepest, darkest secrets when we started the club," Becca said.

"You tell us your secret," I said. "Then we'll tell ours."

"And there's one more rule you should know about," Monica added. "If one of us **accidentally** or **on purpose** tells someone's secret, the others can blab that person's secret."

Adam gasped. "Seriously?"

We all nodded.

Actually, Becca, Monica, and I tell each other everything because we're friends. We would never tell anyone else our secrets.

"Okay," Adam said. He stared at the ceiling and rubbed his chin. Then he cleared his throat. "**I'm afraid of dentists.**"

"That's not a secret," Monica said. "Everyone hates going to the dentist."

"Oh, yeah. I guess so." Adam stared at the floor. Then he looked up suddenly and said, **"I had head lice at camp when I was six."**

"That's not a deep, dark secret," I pointed out.

"You'll have to do better than that," Monica said.

Adam threw up his hands. "But I don't want to tell you my **deepest, darkest secret.**"

"We don't want to tell you our deepest, darkest secrets, either," I said. "But **those are the rules.**"

"Then I can't join the **Whatever Club,**" Adam said. He looked disappointed, but he wasn't mad.

Good thing for me! I didn't want to feel guilty because my idea made Adam quit.

"We're sorry," Becca said.

"So am I," Adam said. "I've been a jerk."

Becca, Monica, and I were speechless.

"I thought it was unfair when you all voted to read magazines," Adam explained. "But I was making you vote for things you didn't want to do."

"We liked some of it." Becca always tries to make people feel better. "I had fun playing baseball."

"Me, too," Monica said.

Then I had another BRILLIANT idea. "There's no rule against doing something we've never done before. We just have to agree."

"Agree on what?" Monica asked.

"We can make Adam an **honorary member,**" I said. "We'll tell him the code word for every meeting. Then he can decide if he wants to come or not."

"That's a GREAT idea!" Becca beamed.

"But honorary members don't vote," I said.

"And they don't have to tell a secret," Monica added.

"I'm in if you guys want me," Adam said.

"All in favor?" I asked.

The vote was UNANIMOUS. We made Adam an **honorary member** of the **Whatever Club.**

"Can we drink the sodas and eat the brownies now?" Becca asked.

"If I had a vote, I'd vote yes," Adam said with a grin.

"Yes!" Monica, Becca, and I shouted.

CHAPTER 13

P.S.

As Becca predicted, Peter and Tommy were not Glory Guys for long. **They didn't like being bossed around.** In fact, all the boys quit when Anna told them that they had to take 𝔹𝔸𝕃𝕃ℝ𝕆𝕆𝕄 **dancing lessons.**

Anna told Tommy that his pranks and jokes were childish. He decided he wouldn't like Anna even if she liked him. She didn't. That was just a rumor.

Tommy did not find out that Becca sort of likes him more than a friend. They're still friends, and **Becca still giggles when he goofs around.**

Adam, Peter, and Tommy helped the **Whatever Club** water seal the tree house. As a thank you, we treated them to a picnic in the park.

Adam comes to meetings when we bake cookies or watch TV. He doesn't come to the monthly **Mag** meeting or when I babysit Nick.

One thing still bugs me, though. **What's the deep, dark secret Adam didn't want to tell us?**

The End

About the Author

Diana G. Gallagher lives in Florida with her husband and five dogs, four cats, and a cranky parrot. Her hobbies are gardening, garage sales, and grandchildren. She has been an English equitation instructor, a professional folk musician, and an artist. However, she had aspirations to be a professional writer at the age of twelve. She has written dozens of books for kids and young adults.

About the Illustrator

Brann Garvey grew up in the great state of Iowa, where he studied art and visual communications. He graduated from the Minneapolis College of Art and Design with a degree in illustration. Brann is usually found with one or more of the following: a pencil in his hand, a comic book, a remote for watching DVDs, or his pet kitty, Iggy. When the weather is nice, Brann likes to play disc golf, and he proudly points out that Iowa is one of the world's centers for the sport. Iggy does not play.

Glossary

accidentally (ak-si-DEN-tuh-lee)—done without meaning to

dominoes (DOM-uh-noz)—a game played with small rectangular tiles

gossip (GOSS-ip)—talk about someone else's personal business

honorary (OH-nuh-rare-ee)—if a person is an honorary member, they are not a full member

initiation (i-nish-ee-AY-shun)—a ceremony that brings someone new into a group

permanent (PUR-muh-nuhnt)—lasting forever

popular (POP-yuh-lur)—if someone is popular, he or she has a lot of friends

postpone (pohst-PONE)—to put something off until a later time

romance (ROH-manss)—a loving relationship

rumor (ROO-mur)—something said by many people. A rumor may or may not be true.

tantrum (TAN-truhm)—an outburst of anger

unanimous (yoo-NAN-uh-muhss)—agreed on by everyone

Discussion Questions

1. Claudia and her friends began the Whatever Club when they weren't asked to be part of the Glory Girls. Has a similar thing ever happened to you? If not, can you think of a similar story in a book or a movie? How did, or would, you handle it? What do you think about how Claudia handled it?

2. Claudia says that some of her interests changed as she grew up. When you were younger, what were your interests? Now that you're older, what are your interests? How are they different? What things have changed?

3. What do you think Claudia's biggest challenge was in this book? Talk about the different challenges she had and how she solved them.

Writing Prompts

1. Have you ever been in Adam's shoes and felt that a friend was leaving you behind? What did you do about it? If it's never happened to you, what do you think you would do in Adam's situation? Write about it.

2. Claudia, Becca, and Monica do a lot of things at their club meetings. Make a list of fun activities that they might do at future meetings. Don't forget to give each meeting its own secret code word!

3. In this book, Claudia and Adam have a problem. They used to be best friends. They did everything together, but they've grown apart. Have you ever had that experience, or known someone who had? What do you think Claudia and Adam could have done to repair their friendship? Write about it.

MORE FUN
with Claudia!

Claudia Cristina Cortez

Just like every other thirteen-year-old girl, Claudia Cristina Cortez has a complicated life. Whether she's studying for the big Quiz Show, babysitting her neighbor, Nick, avoiding mean Jenny Pinski, planning the seventh-grade dance, or trying desperately to pass the swimming test at camp, Claudia goes through her complicated life with confidence, cleverness, and a serious dash of cool.

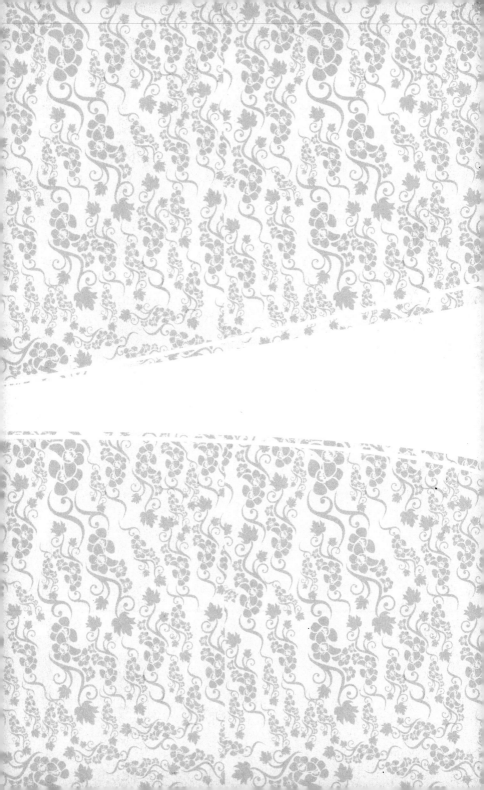